Also by Roy A. Gallant

PRIVATE LIVES OF THE STARS

THE MACMILLAN BOOK OF ASTRONOMY

101 QUESTIONS AND ANSWERS ABOUT THE UNIVERSE

THE PLANETS: Exploring the Solar System

MEMORY: How It Works and How to Improve It

THE CONSTELLATIONS: How They Came to Be

EARTH'S CHANGING CLIMATE

BEYOND EARTH: The Search for Extraterrestrial Life

HOW LIFE BEGAN: Creation vs. Evolution

FIRES IN THE SKY: The Birth and Death of Stars

RAINBOWS·MIRAGES AND SUNDOGS

The Sky as a Source of Wonder

RAINBOWS·MIRAGES AND SUNDOGS

The Sky as a
Source of Wonder

ROY A. GALLANT

MACMILLAN PUBLISHING COMPANY
New York

COLLIER MACMILLAN PUBLISHERS
London

PICTURE CREDITS

Pages 5, 6, 8, 10, 16, 17, 19, 21, 42, 43, 49, 53, 67, 69, 73, 74, 80 (top), 83, illustrations copyright © 1987 by Andrew Mudryk; title page, pages 37, 52, 80 (bottom), photographs by Roy A. Gallant; page 36, courtesy of General Electric Company; pages 44, 60, 76, 77, courtesy of NASA; pages 47, 57, courtesy of NOAA; page 54, courtesy of the Zentral Bibliothek, Zurich; page 66, courtesy of Cathie Polgreen; page 84, courtesy of Lick Observatory. All picture research by Science Photo/Graphics, Inc.

Macmillan Publishing Company
866 Third Avenue, New York, NY 10022
Collier Macmillan Canada, Inc.
Book design by Constance Ftera
First Edition
Printed in the United States of America

10 9 8 7 6 5 4 3 2

The text of this book is set in 12 point Sabon.

Library of Congress Cataloging-in-Publication Data
Gallant, Roy A.
Rainbows, mirages, and sundogs.
Summary: Discusses and explains visual phenomena seen in the sky, primarily interactions of light and atmosphere such as rainbows, the twinkling of stars, the blue color of the sky, and the Northern Lights.
1. Meteorological optics — Juvenile literature.
[1. Meteorological optics] I. Title.
QC975.3.G45   1987   551.56   86-23728
IBN 0-02-737010-0

For Jacqui

ACKNOWLEDGMENTS

This book began as a vague idea many years ago and only gradually took shape as what you now see before you. To say exactly when or how the idea came about initially is impossible. However, I owe my special gratitude to two gentlemen, both physicists. One is Sir William Bragg, whose book *The Universe of Light* has been a constant companion over the years I have been writing science books. The other is Professor M. Minnaert, whose book *The Nature of Light & Colour* has been equally important to me over the years. I wish also to thank Dr. Henry Albers, friend, colleague, and astronomer at Vassar College, Poughkeepsie, New York, for reading the manuscript of this book for accuracy.

CONTENTS

"Without a sense of wonder, the mind would starve."

—Hans Christian von Baeyer

HOW TO CATCH
A RAINBOW

I recently returned from a two-week cruise in the Caribbean aboard the *Bermuda Star*, where I lectured on astronomy and led nightly observing sessions of Halley's Comet. Each evening, more than 100 people turned out as we watched the little fuzz-ball comet creep its way westward across the sky.

I was surprised by the large number of people who, beneath that clear sky free of pollution and the glare of city lights, marveled at the stars they could see. Several said that never in their lives had they seen so many stars. Others had never seen the Milky Way before, then a strikingly bright band of stars glowing in the southeastern sky. Some said that it was the first time that they had recognized a planet, and one asked why the Moon appeared small and pale when high overhead but sometimes large and orange when near the horizon.

As each of those balmy nights wore on into the early hours, the night vision of my comet watchers improved, and still more marvels of the sky were revealed to them. A galaxy in Centaurus, an easy binocular object, soon became an old friend instantly spotted on following nights. Sirius in the early-evening sky shone a brilliant blue-white and rivaled yellow-white Venus. Antares in Scorpius flickered with a strong reddish light, while nearby Saturn shone with a steadier blue-green light.

By the middle of the first week, many of the same people began appearing on deck each night, eager for their "awareness therapy," as one doctor from Chicago put it. After watching the comet for fifteen minutes or so, they wanted me to point out other things to see in the sky. "Help me look," said a social worker from New Orleans. "It is all so very beautiful and mysterious."

That, in essence, is what this book is about, a way to help you look at the sky — both during the day and night — and discover things you perhaps never realized could be seen, or things you have seen before but never understood.

So join me on this cruise across the sky. I will take you through a rainbow and show you how to make a rainbow of your own. We will build mirages and then watch them dissolve before our eyes; find that cloud with a silver lining; watch the sky as it is bathed in the shimmering curtains of the Northern Lights. We will find out why the stars twinkle, why the Moon turns red during a lunar eclipse, and why the sky is blue instead of green. So come with me and let me help you look, for "it is all so very beautiful and mysterious."

Roy A. Gallant
May 1986

1
CHASING RAINBOWS

You've probably seen lots of rainbows. But have you ever wondered what a rainbow really is and what causes one? How many of the following questions about rainbows can you answer?

Do you think you can see a rainbow in the summer around noon? What band of color forms the top of a rainbow? Can you walk up to one end of a rainbow, where the pot of gold is hidden? Can you grab onto a small rainbow and move it around? Can you ever see a rainbow as a complete circle? Can there ever be a double rainbow?

Long ago, people used to be afraid of rainbows, thinking that they were snakes that rose up into the sky to drink water. And superstitious people warned that you must never point at a rainbow. If you did, you could lose your finger.

Today, rainbows are no longer objects of fear but things of beauty. Becoming an expert rainbow watcher will make you appreciate these wonders of colors in the sky. Usually we see rainbows after a rain shower or in the fine spray of a fountain or waterfall.

The bands of color form a perfect half circle. But if you happen to be flying in an airplane and see a rainbow, it will take the shape of a full circle with the shadow of the plane in the center.

From the top edge of the rainbow to the bottom, the order of color bands is always red, orange, yellow, green, blue, and violet. But the brightness of this or that color band, and its width, may change from one minute to the next, and from one rainbow to another. This collection of color bands is called the primary rainbow.

Sometimes you can see a double rainbow, with a second rainbow curving above the primary rainbow. And if you look carefully, you will see that the order of the color bands is backward in the second rainbow. Also notice that a darker band of sky divides the two rainbows. That narrow, darker band was first reported by a rainbow watcher named Alexander about 2,000 years ago.

If you look still harder, you will notice that the sky framed by the inside of the primary rainbow is lighter than the outer sky. Sometimes you can even see faint bands of pink and green there. The sky looks paler in that region because the light that forms the blue-violet band at the bottom of the rainbow is bent and spread around more than the light that forms the red band at the top.

About 2,000 years ago, the famous Greek scholar Aristotle said that a rainbow is not an object that we can touch in space. Instead, it is a series of places in the sky where we see light spread out, or scattered. Where we see those places of light scattering depends on where we are standing in relation to the Sun. As we move about, a rainbow tags along with us, just as the Moon seems to follow us as we walk.

You will find that a morning rainbow always is off toward the west with the Sun behind you. Afternoon rainbows always are in the east, again with the Sun behind you. What happens to a sum-

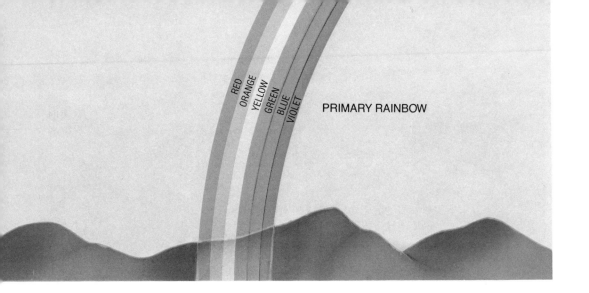

RED
ORANGE
YELLOW
GREEN
BLUE
VIOLET

PRIMARY RAINBOW

Above: *The colors of a single, or primary, rainbow result from white light being separated into its full array of colors. From top to bottom of a primary rainbow, the colors are red, orange, yellow, green, blue, and violet. The colors may be bright or faint but always appear in the same order. Below: Sometimes we see a double rainbow. The color bands in the upper and fainter rainbow are in reverse order, with red at the bottom and violet at top. The top edge of the primary rainbow forms an angle of 42 degrees; the top edge of the secondary rainbow forms an angle of 50 degrees.*

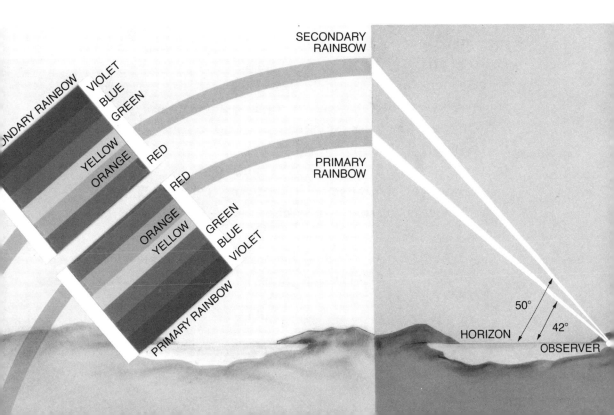

SECONDARY RAINBOW

SECONDARY RAINBOW

VIOLET
BLUE
GREEN
YELLOW
ORANGE
RED

RED
ORANGE
YELLOW
GREEN
BLUE
VIOLET

PRIMARY RAINBOW

PRIMARY RAINBOW

50°
42°
HORIZON
OBSERVER

Nail a piece of white cardboard to a pole and sight along the top edge to the top of the rainbow. The card's top edge and the shadow cast by the nail form an angle of 42 degrees. As the Sun moves up or down the sky, that angle does not change, showing that a rainbow moves as the Sun moves.

mer-morning rainbow as the Sun inches its way higher above the horizon? You can find out with the aid of a 3-by-5-inch file card.

Use a long, thin nail to pin the 3-by-5-inch card to a tree at about eye level and then sight along the top long edge of the card to the top of the rainbow. With the card in that position, trace a line along the shadow cast by the nail. If you draw that line off the top edge of the card, it will form an angle of 42 degrees with the top edge. The angle always remains the same, which means that as the Sun moves up or down the sky, so does a rainbow move right along with the Sun.

Every rainbow is an arc, or part of a complete circle. The line you draw on your card points to the center of the rainbow circle. So a line drawn from the Sun through where you are standing points to the very center of the rainbow.

Say that you see a rainbow at sunrise. The center of the rainbow will be on the western horizon, so you will see exactly one half of the rainbow circle. Later, as the Sun climbs higher, the rainbow gradually lowers toward the horizon. When the Sun climbs to a height of 42 degrees above the horizon (nearly halfway up the sky), the top edge of the rainbow slips from view below the horizon. The rainbow is gone.

Just the opposite happens in the afternoon. You cannot see an afternoon rainbow until the Sun has lowered to 42 degrees above the western horizon. You will then see the top edge of the rainbow rising over the eastern horizon. As the Sun sinks lower, the arc of the rainbow grows larger and larger. At sunset, the rainbow is once again a half circle resting on the horizon, and its top is 42 degrees above the horizon.

What Is a Rainbow?

We see a rainbow when the Sun's light is refracted, or bent, on passing through tiny rain droplets falling in the air. We cannot follow the arc of a rainbow down below the horizon, because we cannot see those droplets in the air below the horizon. But the higher we are above the ground, the more of the rainbow circle we will see. That's why, from an airplane in flight, a rainbow will appear as a complete circle with the shadow of the airplane in the center.

Have you ever played with a prism? A prism is a three-sided block of glass or plastic. When a beam of sunlight shines through a prism, something interesting happens to the light. It is separated

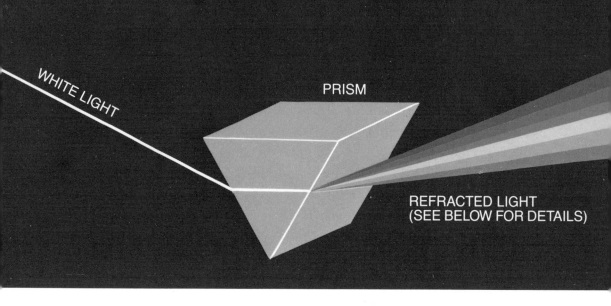

WHITE LIGHT

PRISM

REFRACTED LIGHT
(SEE BELOW FOR DETAILS)

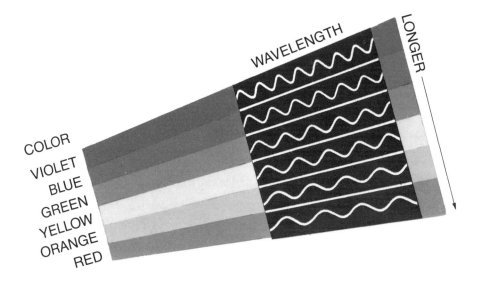

WAVELENGTH

LONGER

COLOR
VIOLET
BLUE
GREEN
YELLOW
ORANGE
RED

A prism breaks white light into its full array of colors. Since each color has a certain wavelength, the colors always are in the same order. Colors of shorter wavelength are refracted most.

into a display of colors arranged in the same order as the colors in a rainbow. So sunlight, which appears to be white, really is made up of a mixture of red, orange, yellow, green, blue, and violet light. A prism unscrambles those colors. You can think of each color of light as a train of waves. Violet light, at one edge of a prism's display of colors, has the shortest waves, or wavelength. Red, at the opposite edge, has the longest wavelength. So, moving from the violet edge of a rainbow through the colors to red at the opposite edge, the wavelengths get longer. Since the shorter wavelengths of light are refracted more than the longer wavelengths, the color bands of a rainbow always have the same order of colors—red, orange, yellow, green, blue, and violet. Now, what happens to unscramble the Sun's light and produce a rainbow in the sky?

When it is raining, each tiny droplet of water in the air acts as a prism, even though it has the shape of a ball. When a beam of sunlight passes through the curved surface of a raindrop prism, it is separated and spread out into the familiar bands of color. Once a light beam enters a water droplet, it bounces off the rear surface and exits the droplet through the forward surface. As it does, the light beam gets refracted a second time. This second bending fans out the colors even more. In this way, each individual water droplet makes its own primary rainbow. Because there are millions upon millions of water droplets spread all over the sky, we see a large single rainbow.

Sometimes we can see a double rainbow, a fainter one above a brighter one. What causes this second rainbow? Some of the light entering a water droplet is bounced off the inner wall twice before exiting the droplet. A light beam reflected twice produces a second rainbow. Since some of the light escapes on the second trip around the inside of a droplet, the colors in these secondary rainbows are

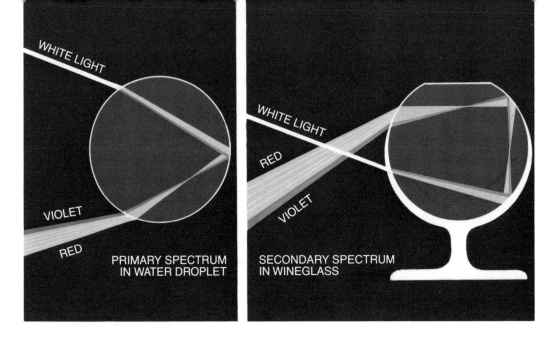

WHITE LIGHT

VIOLET

RED

PRIMARY SPECTRUM
IN WATER DROPLET

WHITE LIGHT

RED

VIOLET

SECONDARY SPECTRUM
IN WINEGLASS

A water droplet (left) *acts as a prism that refracts and reflects light. It refracts a light beam once on entering the drop, then again on exiting. In a water glass "raindrop," a light beam is reflected twice before exiting.*

fainter than the colors in a primary rainbow. A secondary rainbow is about 8 degrees higher in the sky than the primary because the light forming it exits from the water droplets at a different angle. And the bands of color are reversed because the color fan is flip-flopped during the second trip around the inside of the water droplet. You can expect to see double rainbows when the sunlight is strong and the water droplets are small.

A WINEGLASS RAINDROP

A wineglass, or any similarly rounded glass, makes a good experimental raindrop. But a tall, straight-sided glass will work just as well. While the wineglass gives a spot of color in this experiment, a straight-sided glass gives a line of color.

Fill the glass with water, but not too full, since you'll be moving it around in the air. In a darkened room, place a flashlight flat on some object about as high as your shoulder. Standing with your back to the flashlight, hold the glass by the bottom and out at arm's length straight ahead of you. Then move the glass to the left over a distance of about one foot until you see some colors. You may see a splash of colors at first, but the color you are looking for is a bright red line near the side of the glass. It is a reflection off the far inside curved surface of the glass. The first many-colored splash you may have seen was a reflection off the near outside curved surface of the glass.

As with a real raindrop reflecting and refracting light from the Sun, your water-glass "raindrop" reflects and bends light from the flashlight. The flashlight beam of white light enters the glass of water, is reflected off the inside curved surface, and shines through the water to your eye. On entering the water, the beam is refracted, and it is refracted again on leaving the water. In this position, all colors except red are bent so much that they are out of your sight. Red remains visible because it is refracted least.

If you move the glass slightly in one direction, the red line disappears. Move it slightly in the opposite direction, and a color other than red appears. Try arranging a half circle of small, water-filled glasses around you. Since you will be viewing each glass from a different angle, you will see a different color in each one. The colors will range from blue at one end to red at the other end of your half circle—a complete water-glass rainbow!

If you are lucky enough to see a rainbow at sunset, you may be in for a rare treat—an all-red rainbow. Such a sunset rainbow may linger in the sky for ten minutes after sunset. Usually, a rainbow fades out gradually until only a bright rim of red is left. What happens is that, as the Sun lowers, it shines through a deeper and deeper amount of air. This increased crowding of air molecules causes the shorter wavelengths of light to be scattered so widely that you can no longer see them. Only the longer, red wavelengths are left to form the red rainbow.

Maybe you've heard the weather saying: "Rainbow at night, sailor's delight; rainbow at morning, sailor take warning." This is generally true in the mid-latitudes where weather moves from west to east. In the morning, with the Sun behind you, a rainbow can mean that bad weather is moving in your direction from the west. At dusk, when the Sun is behind you, a rainbow can mean that bad weather is moving away from you.

Fogbows and Dewbows

Fogbows are special. The very small size of fog droplets causes an unusual bow. You can see fogbows best from a hilltop with the fog in front and below, and with the Sun behind you. You will see a white band twice the size of an ordinary rainbow. It has a rim of orange at the top and a rim of pale blue at the bottom. You may even see one or two extra arcs of red-green-red-green tucked inside the bow. Some fogbows are caused by ordinary streetlights, but to see them there must be a dark background.

There also are dewbows. They may appear on an autumn morning before the Sun is high and when a field or lawn is covered with cobwebs of dew. The bow lies flat on the ground and curves off in the shape of part of a stretched-out circle.

Have you ever seen a Moonbow? These are rainbows caused by

the Moon instead of the Sun. Because the Moon's reflected light is so much fainter than sunlight, the Moon must be full and bright to cast a bow. As the colors of objects seen in moonlight look washed-out and grayish, so is a Moonbow colorless, appearing only as a hazy rim of whitish light. Don't mistake a Moonbow for a ring around the Moon (see pages 46–57). The two are different.

You can see rainbows in many different kinds of weather conditions. Some will be especially colorful, others dull in color, some bright, others dim. One way you can learn more about rainbows is to make your own.

PERSONAL RAINBOWS FOR HOME USE

With a garden hose you can create many kinds of homegrown personal rainbows. You need a hose with a nozzle that you can turn to change the size of the water drops. Pick a clear day when the Sun is bright. Be sure to have the Sun behind you and not higher in the sky than 42 degrees, or a little less than halfway up the sky.

Spray the water on the finest spray setting of the nozzle and wave the hose around until you see a rainbow. You'll even be able to make a complete-circle rainbow. Move around a bit and see what the rainbow does. Is it fixed in one place in the air? Do you see two rainbows crossing each other? If so, wink your eyes back and forth. Each eye should see its own rainbow. Aim the hose so that you see a secondary rainbow with extra arcs. Keep experimenting by changing the hose jet to alter the size of the water droplets. What happens to the rainbow? Have someone photograph the rainbows as you make them. Are you surprised that you can photograph a rainbow?

2
MIRAGE: NOW YOU SEE IT...

The year was 1818. The Scottish explorer Sir John Ross was searching for a way to sail from the Atlantic Ocean near Greenland, then across through the Arctic Ocean and into the Pacific Ocean. If such a "northwest passage" through ice-choked Arctic waters could be found, it would save trading ships from Europe thousands of miles of needless travel into the South Atlantic and all the way around the tip of South America.

When his ship was in Lancaster Sound, Ross saw, off in the distance, what appeared to be a range of mountains blocking his way. He decided to turn back. If there were a northwest passage across the Arctic, he thought, it could not be through Lancaster Sound. Ross was wrong. The mountain range he saw was not there at all. It was a mirage, that bending of light rays that tricks the eye into seeing something that isn't there.

In the year 1906, the American explorer Robert E. Peary was on his way to discover the North Pole. He reported a grand view of "snow-clad summits above the ice horizon" from his position at Cape Thomas Hubbard. Later, he saw the mountains again, this time from Ellesmere Island. But it was too late in the season to travel farther north. With a heavy heart, he knew that he must turn back and leave the exploration of those grand, snow-capped peaks to another man.

Seven years later, the American explorer Donald B. MacMillan set out to explore those peaks reported by Peary and called "Crocker Land." He had no trouble finding them. There they were in clear sight, perhaps 30 miles ahead. MacMillan wrote: "There could be no doubt about it. Great heavens, what a land! Hills, valleys, snow-capped peaks [stretching halfway across] the horizon." After hiking over the Arctic ice for about 30 miles, MacMillan looked again and then blinked in disbelief. Crocker Land simply melted from view. It was a mirage. Those mountains, valleys, and hills that Peary and MacMillan had seen did not exist.

What Makes a Mirage?

Since a mirage can be photographed, it is not "all in the mind." If it isn't in the mind, and if it isn't "up there ahead," then where is it? And what is it? A mirage is the image of an object, not the object itself. When we see a distant object, we usually look directly at it. But when we see a mirage of an object, the object usually is not in our direct line of sight. If that is so, then how can we see the image of the object? As you read these words, light from the book page travels through the air straight from the page to your eyes. But when you are outside and see an object far away, the light shining off that object and traveling to your eyes sometimes gets refracted as it passes through the air to your eyes. At such times, you may see an object that really isn't where it appears to be.

Riding along the highway, maybe you have noticed what appears to be a patch of dark and shining water in the road ahead. Travelers crossing the desert also have "seen" ponds or lakes shimmering off in the distance. But the traveler can never manage to reach the water. It just keeps moving away as he walks toward it. Or it gradually vanishes before the eyes.

When the air temperature near the surface is higher than the air temperature above, you may see that mirage of a refreshing pond in the middle of a desert, or the puddle of water on the highway ahead. This happens when the highway or desert sand heats up quickly in the early morning after a cool night. The hot land surface then warms the air just above it. Because hot air is thinner than cool air, light from an object shining through a parcel of air hot at the bottom and cool at the top is refracted unevenly. If light from a patch of blue sky near the horizon is refracted, the patch of sky may

The "puddle" mirage you see on the road ahead or on the desert is caused by hot air just above the surface of the ground. The air refracts the light from a distant patch of sky in such a way that the patch appears to be on the ground ahead of you rather than in the sky above.

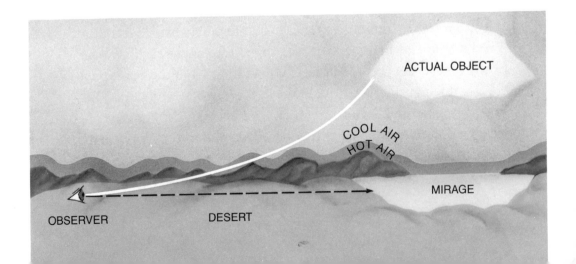

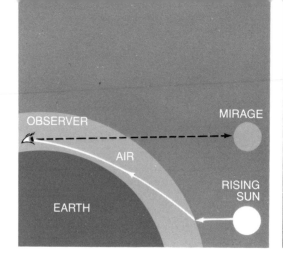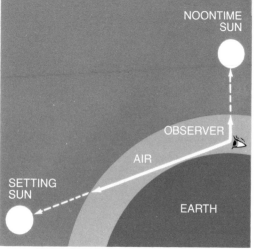

Left: *Our first glimpse of the Sun at sunrise is a mirage. While the Sun still is below the horizon, sunlight refracted on passing through the air to our eyes makes the Sun appear to be above the horizon, even though the Sun has not yet arrived in that position.* Right: *An early morning or late afternoon Sun creates more interesting effects for us to see than does a noonday Sun. The reason is that at sunrise and sunset the Sun's rays pass through a greater thickness of air than they do at noon.*

appear to be down on the ground—as that desert pond or highway puddle—instead of up in the sky where it belongs.

Stooping down to get a lower sighting of the mirage will give you a much clearer view of it. You nearly always have a better view of a mirage from sea level than from a hilltop. For example, a person on the deck of a ship at sea may see a mirage of an island off in the distance, while a crew member up in the rigging will not see the "island."

As surprising as it may seem, the first glimpse of the Sun at sunrise and the last glimpse at sunset are examples of mirages. At sunrise, the Sun appears to be moving up over the horizon, or, at sunset, to be slipping down below the horizon. But actually, at sunrise we see an image of the Sun on the horizon before the Sun actually reaches it. And at sunset we continue to see an image of the Sun briefly after the Sun actually has set. How can that be so?

The light from a rising or setting Sun passes through a greater thickness of Earth's air than the noontime sunlight does. The refracted sunlight from a rising or setting Sun is what causes us to see an image of the Sun above the horizon before the Sun actually reaches that position. The refracted light also sometimes causes the Sun to appear a bit flattened when near the horizon.

Ever heard of the "Moon illusion"? You probably have noticed that when the Moon is full and just coming up over the horizon it appears much larger than when you see it directly overhead. This apparent difference in size has nothing to do with refraction but seems to be caused by our being able to see the Moon in close relation to features of the landscape. When higher, the full Moon seems smaller because it is not seen in relation to other and familiar objects. The next time you see a full Moon rise over the horizon in early evening, watch it for 20 minutes or more. It will appear to become smaller as it climbs higher.

Here's a question that most people answer incorrectly: Which object, when held at arm's length away from your eye, most exactly covers the full Moon when about halfway up the sky—a tennis ball, a golf ball, a quarter, a penny, or a pea? Try it and find out.

"Looming" Mirages

The magnification effect of Earth's air has caused some interesting, and amusing, mirages. For example, if you live by the seacoast, maybe you have seen a distant ship look as though it had been stretched upward. When air conditions are just right, the ship may also seem to be gliding along just above the water. People who work at sea call this a "looming" mirage. It occurs when the air

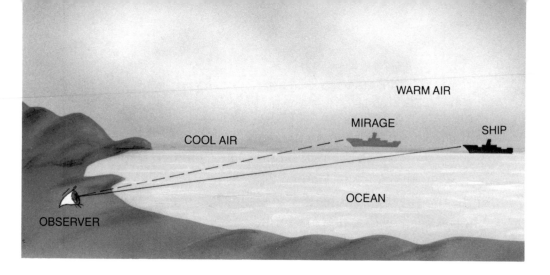

In a "looming" mirage, a distant ship may appear to be sailing along above the water. This happens when light from the ship is refracted through air made up of a warm layer resting above a cool layer. Looming mirages, which may magnify the real object, are the only mirages that appear to be nearby.

temperature just above the water surface is lower than the air temperature higher up. This causes light from the top of the ship to be bent more than light coming from the base of the ship at the waterline, and so the ship appears to be stretched up.

Looming mirages are the only mirages that appear to be nearby. They also may greatly magnify the real object. Because of a looming mirage, the polar explorer Fridtjof Nansen once nearly shot one of his sled dogs, thinking it was a polar bear. Another time, a ship's captain off Newfoundland saw what he thought was a white motorboat ahead. Just as he was about to turn his ship to avoid ramming the boat, the boat flapped its wings and flew away. It was a looming mirage of a sea gull magnified several times, as Nansen's dog had been.

A number of years ago, the crew of a Canadian ship in the Arctic reported an interesting mirage. They clearly saw a sailing ship off in the distance, upside-down. The image was so sharp that the crew could make out the ropes in the rigging, and they could see people moving about on deck. Two months later, the two ships actually met. When the captains compared their ships' logs, they found that at the time of the sighting the two ships had been 80 miles apart. Mirages such as that one are formed when a layer of warm air is sandwiched between two layers of cooler and denser air.

HOW TO MEASURE THE HORIZON

If you live near the sea or near a big lake that stretches off to the horizon, you can measure the ups and downs of the horizon by using a short stick and a long stick.

The short stick should be about 4 feet long. Pound it into the sand above the high-tide mark if you are by the sea, or 10 feet or so up the beach from the waterline if you are by a large lake. The second "stick" can be a tree or telephone pole about 100 yards away from the stick. Pick a time in the morning when the air is cool. Make a mark on the long stick about the height of your shoulder. With your eye at the level of the mark, sight over the top of the short stick to the distant horizon. Now have someone adjust the height of the short stick so that its top appears even with the horizon.

Your experiment is now set up, and you have made your first measurement—the mark on the long stick showing alignment of the top of the short stick and the horizon. Now wait a few hours for the air temperature to change, then sight again. Leave the short stick just the way it was for your first measurement. Begin with your eye at the level of the mark you made on the long stick. Notice

Depending on the difference in temperature of the surface water of the ocean and the air just above, the horizon may appear higher or lower at a given time. Arranging two sticks as shown here (and explained in the text), you can measure the apparent ups and downs of the horizon throughout the day.

that the top of the short stick is no longer aligned with the horizon. Move your head up or down until the top of the short stick is aligned with the horizon, then make a second mark at eye level on the long stick.

If it is early morning or around sunset, the air probably will be cooler than the water. You will find that the new mark will be about 7 to 12 inches lower than your first mark. What has happened is that the light reaching your eyes from the horizon has been bent so that the horizon now appears higher than before.

Next, wait until high noon, when the air is hotter than the water, and make another sighting. The mark you make this time will be several inches higher than the second mark. The light from the horizon this time is bent the opposite way.

Totem-Pole Mirages

When there is more than one hot-air sandwich, we may see two or more mirages at once. In the case of the upside-down sailing boat, the crew might have seen the mirage-boat standing on its masts just above the water, then on top of that mirage a second mirage of the boat, but this one right side up, and then another upside-down boat on top of the second one—a totem pole of sailing boats.

A wind can blow away a mirage because it mixes the hot and cold air layers. Or the mirage will go away if the Sun heats the air so that there is no longer a layering of thin, warm air and of dense, cool air. Most mirages last only a short time, but there are exceptions. Labrador is a land of mirages in summer. The cause is a cold ocean current that flows down on Labrador's coast. In summer the land heats up, so there is a layer of warm air near the ground topped by a layer of cold air. This condition is ideal for the sighting of island mirages; some Labrador mirages are so regular and dependable that ships can navigate by them.

Mirages seldom are so useful, as in the case of Peary and Mac-Millan. MacMillan's Crocker Land of hills, valleys, and beautiful snow-capped peaks was one of the most spectacular types of mirages. It is called a *fata morgana*, Italian for the Fairy Morgan, also known as Morgan le Fay, who appears in the legends of King Arthur and was known for her magical power to create castles in the air. This kind of fantastically detailed image is caused by light refracted from a featureless landscape of barren snow or water.

3
TWINKLE, TWINKLE, ANY STAR

On a summer evening just after sunset, watch the sky as the stars twinkle into view. As the sky darkens, the brighter stars appear first, then the fainter ones. Within a half hour it is dark. If you have not looked at a bright light in this time, your eyes have become adjusted to the night. You are dark adapted, which means that your eyes gradually have adjusted to let in more light. You now have your night vision. So that they will not lose their night vision, astronomers do not use ordinary flashlights when taking notes or making adjustments to their telescopes. Instead, they use a red light, which has little effect on night vision.

If you take the time to relax for an hour or so under the night sky, you will marvel at the many stars that you can see and that you can find with the aid of a star chart. This is especially so away from city lights, where the sky is dark. One thing you will notice is that all the stars appear to move as a group, rising in the east and setting in the west. But this apparent motion is a trick motion caused by Earth's rotation, or spinning around like a top. You also will notice that the stars seem to twinkle. This flickering doesn't happen in the stars themselves, but is caused by the layers of air we must look through to see the stars.

Air and Scintillation

The scientific name for twinkling is scintillation. Stars low on the horizon seem to twinkle more than those high overhead. Also, those near the horizon may appear to change color from time to time as they dance about and flash. They may also seem to change in size, brightness, or position, sometimes quite quickly. The reason that more of these changes can be seen in the sky down near the horizon, rather than high overhead, is that we are looking through a greater thickness of air when we look toward the horizon than when we look straight up.

Suppose that you are looking at the planet Venus or some bright star close to the horizon, and you see Venus or the star seem to change position. The change may be rapid, or it may be slow. It happens when the light from Venus or the star is bent on passing through a layer of warm air that is next to a layer of cooler air. Remember that air is always in motion. Air layers of different temperatures may be sandwiched together and moving up and down like ocean swells. As a sea gull riding on ocean waves moves up and down with the waves, Venus or the star appears to move up and down, or back and forth, as its light rays pass through air layers of different temperatures and are bent this way and that.

There also are many little whirling packets of air called eddies that usually are not so dense as the surrounding air. As the light rays from a star are refracted many times a second on passing through eddies, the light is bent in fits and starts, and so the star seems to twinkle. In winter, the differences in temperature among layers and packets of air are greater than in summer. This means that the twinkling effect—along with slower changes in apparent brightness—is stronger in cold weather.

Larger parcels of air may be of different temperatures and, therefore, of different densities. Some of these air parcels may be the size of a house or larger. As the light rays from Venus, for instance, pass through one of these air parcels, they may be bunched close together and so appear especially bright for a time. Then, as the wind moves that air parcel along and brings a different one between Venus and you, the light rays may be spread farther apart. This will make Venus appear dimmer than before. Such brightness changes may last for several minutes, and so are different from twinkling.

The differences in temperature, and therefore in density, among neighboring parcels of air also can cause Venus or a star to appear to change color. Sometimes we see Venus as a yellow object, other times orange, and sometimes reddish. When seen close to the horizon, the bright, blue-white winter star Sirius may look like a diamond in the sky, flashing its blue color as air parcels of different temperatures drift past our eyes. At such times, the color of Sirius also may appear to change. Both Venus and Sirius, by the way, during their flashing and color changes have been reported as flying saucers (UFOs) sending signals to us Earthlings!

Most color changing of the planets and stars will be seen below an angle of 35 degrees, which is a little less than halfway up the sky. Few, if any, color changes will be seen above a height of 50 degrees.

Scintillation is best in one or more of these conditions: 1) just before a storm when the barometer is low; 2) when the air is cold; 3) when the humidity is high; or 4) when the wind is moving the air about briskly, but not strongly.

EXPERIMENTING WITH SCINTILLATIONS

You can use a pocket mirror to experiment with scintillations. While looking at a star reflected in the mirror, move the mirror rapidly in small circles three or four times a second. Or find a bright star near the horizon and look at it through binoculars while lightly tapping the binoculars with a finger. What do you see? Do you see any color changes?

While you or I might enjoy the dancing and flashing of planets and bright stars near the horizon, astronomers usually do not. On nights when the air is alive with layers, packets, and parcels of hot and cold air moving about, astronomers say that the "seeing" is poor. If they try to take time-exposure photographs of planets or certain stars under these conditions, their photographs will be blurred and appear out of focus. That is why the big telescopes are built high on mountaintops, above most of the dense and warmer air. A mountaintop telescope will have better seeing conditions because there is less air, and less disturbed air, to peer through than there is at sea level.

4
WHY IS THE SKY BLUE?

Planet Earth sometimes is called the "blue planet." Whether we look from a mountaintop, from an ocean liner, or from an airplane, the sky appears blue when there are no clouds. And when the astronauts look back to Earth from space, the planet also appears blue. Its color largely is due to the reflection of blue light from the sky by ocean water. But when the astronauts turn their eyes away from Earth, the sky of space is black. Why should Earth's sky be blue and the sky of space black?

Not only is our sky blue, but it ranges over many shades of blue. It also changes its blue tint from one time to another and from one part of the sky to another. This blue light cannot come from the air itself, since at night the blue sky "goes out" with the Sun. Skylight must, then, be caused by the Sun by day and much less by the Moon at night. But as seen from Earth's surface, the Sun is yellowish white and the Moon—which acts like a dull mirror reflecting light from the Sun—is mostly white, except when both are low on the horizon.

We can now sharpen our question and ask *how* light from the Sun can make the sky blue. To find the answer, we must discover what happens to sunlight as it shines down through Earth's air.

A Look at Earth's Air

We live at the bottom of an ocean of air that stretches above us to a height of about 300 miles and that is made up of many different gases. Most of Earth's air (78 percent) is a gas called nitrogen. When we take a breathe, we breathe in nitrogen. But our bodies don't use the nitrogen so we breathe it right back out again. Most of the rest of the air (21 percent) is oxygen. Our bodies do use oxygen. In fact, if we did not have oxygen to breathe we would die. Oxygen enters our lungs and is carried to all other parts of our body by our blood. At the same time, our blood unloads a poisonous waste gas called carbon dioxide into our lungs, and we breathe out that gas when we exhale. So the air contains small amounts of carbon dioxide as well. It also contains small amounts of other gases, including argon, neon, and several more.

The gases of the air come in small bundles called molecules. Molecules are made up of one or more smaller particles called atoms. For example, an oxygen molecule is made up of two atoms of oxygen (written O_2). A nitrogen molecule also is made up of two atoms (N_2). A carbon dioxide molecule is made up of one atom of carbon and two atoms of oxygen (CO_2).

But the air contains more than those gases. Erupting volcanoes, such as Mount Saint Helens, pour other gases, ash, dust, and soot into the air. Windstorms pick up and add dust and fine sand to the air. And our factories pour tons and tons of smoke and ash into the air each day. So the air is a great mixture of gases and solid particles ranging in size from that of a tiny atom to dust particles large enough to see.

As sunlight shines down through the air, something interesting happens to the light. As its rays move among the gas molecules and dust particles, the rays become scattered, or spread out, much as a fine plume of smoke is spread out as it rises. If you have read the chapter on rainbows, you learned that the white light of the Sun or from a flashlight is made up of different colors: red, orange, yellow, green, blue, and violet (see page 9). We can see each of those individual colors by passing a beam of sunlight through a prism.

To understand how we can separate the individual colors from sunlight, you must know something else about light. As light travels along through space or through the air, it moves as a wave moves. Some of the colors (violet and blue) have short waves, or wavelengths, meaning that the distance between wave crests is short. Other colors (orange and red) have long waves, with the distance between wave crests farther apart.

Experiments have shown that the rays of shorter wavelengths are scattered more than the rays of longer wavelengths. So violet and blue are scattered most, followed by some green and yellow, and followed last by orange and a little bit of red. Because the blue wavelengths of color are scattered so widely, the sky appears blue. The blue rays are scattered in all directions, back and forth, up and down. Wherever we look in the sky, we see some of this scattered light and we say that "the sky is blue." At least that is what we see on a clear day after the air has been swept clean of dust and soot by rain. At such times, the distant landscape also appears a bluish violet, the violet color coming from the scattering of the very short violet wavelengths.

The next time you are driving through or near mountains on a clear day, notice how blue the distant peaks appear. Ever heard of the Blue Ridge Mountains that run from Georgia to Virginia? There also is a Mount Blue in Maine. As you drive along on a summer day, notice that a tree near the roadside appears green, the color of its leaves. But a tree a half mile away appears bluish green, and the distant forest landscape appears quite blue on a clear day. The farther away you are from a distant object, the more air there is between you and the object to scatter blue light. That is one reason why the ocean off near the horizon—like those distant mountains—appears so blue. Another reason is that the tiny molecules of water scatter blue light best, just as the tiny air molecules do. And the deeper the sunlight shines down into the ocean, the bluer the water appears.

Waves breaking nearby on the beach appear not blue but greenish. This is because the water contains particles of clay or sand, which are much larger than water molecules. Sunlight shining on these larger particles of matter is reflected back to our eyes. We then see a greenish color because these larger particles of sand and clay scatter the longer wavelengths of green more widely than they scatter the shorter wavelengths of blue. If a quiet, deep pool of blue seawater happens to contain patches of that greenish brown seaweed called rockweed, the color reflected from the seaweed blends with the blue of the water and makes delicate purples.

If you take a trip by air and fly at a height of 30,000 feet or so, notice the deep blue color of the sky. The space-shuttle astronauts see the blue of the sky deepen and darken as they climb to orbital altitude. Once there, they are above Earth's ocean of air, and the sky is no longer blue but black. It is black because there are no air particles or dust particles to scatter sunlight at all. And the Sun appears as an intensely bright, glaring white object, for there is no screen of air to dim or color its rays. Its yellowish tint has gone. And from space, the stars no longer twinkle but appear as bright pinpoints of light shining steadily.

MEASURING THE BLUENESS OF THE SKY

Be a sky watcher and measure the blueness of the sky. You can by doing this: Cut six or so strips of white cardboard about 2 inches wide and 6 inches long. Then, with oil paints or with acrylics, paint each piece of card a different shade of blue by mixing zinc white with different amounts of cobalt blue or Prussian blue. Number your cards from 1 (lightest blue) to 6 (darkest). You can then keep a record of the blueness of the sky from day to day. With your back to the Sun, hold the cards up against the sky and write down the number of the card that is closest to the color of the sky. Also make a note of the weather and air conditions when you make your measurement. Was it hazy? High, thin clouds? A smoggy day? A clear day after a rain?

White Skies and Red Skies

On a clear day, there are not very many large particles of dust, smoke, and fine sand in the air. Most of the air particles are tiny — molecules of nitrogen, oxygen, and other gases. It is these tiny particles of matter in the air that are especially good at scattering sunlight. And, again, it is the blue waves of light that are scattered most. That is why the sky is such a strong blue on a clear day.

But what happens on a day when the air has lots of dust, smoke, and other large particles floating around? At such times, we have only a hazy view of the distant landscape, and the sky appears whitish rather than blue when the Sun is overhead. On days when there are many very high and feathery clouds made up of ice crystals, the midday sky also appears whitish rather than blue. Here is evidence that larger particles—such as dust and smoke grains and ice crystals—in the air are not the ones that scatter blue light best.

When the Sun is on the horizon the colors we see are different. At sunset (as at sunrise), the Sun is near the horizon and so is shining through a greater thickness of air than when it is overhead (see page 18). It also is shining through more of the dust and water vapor that always hang in the air. At such times, all the wavelengths of light except orange and red are scattered so much that their brightness is greatly weakened and so we do not see them. Instead, we see the longer orange-red wavelengths, which are scattered much less and so remain bright.

If you have ever watched a sunset through the smoke and haze of a forest or brushfire, you have seen a sky as red as the flames. In the late 1800s, the volcanic island of Krakatoa blew up and threw millions of tons of fine dust into the air. Global winds carried the dust around the world. For about a year, people in many countries saw spectacular sunsets and sunrises that were strangely beautiful, tinted with green, blue, and other colors. The extremely fine volcanic dust hanging in the air scattered the blue and green wavelengths just enough to make them shine in the early-morning and evening skies. It was the combination of smoke and dust particles in the air and the Sun shining through a greater depth of air at sunrise and sunset that produced the spectacular results.

On the planet Venus, the atmosphere is extremely dense. The atmospheric pressure at Venus's surface is 90 times that of Earth, enough to crush you to death. This superdense air scatters, and so weakens, all but the orange-red wavelengths so much that Venus's entire sky probably appears red from morning to night.

THE SKY IN A FISHBOWL

Try this experiment: Fill a small fishbowl with water and stir in 2 tablespoons of milk. With the room darkened, place a flashlight so that it is lying flat on top of two or three books and shining through the goldfish bowl from about 3 or 4 feet away. Now, with your eyes down at the level of the bowl, look through it with the light behind you. Your water "sky" should appear bluish, due to the scattering of the short wavelengths by the milk particles. Now look through the bowl from a position opposite the flashlight so that you are looking directly into the light. What colors do you see now? Slowly move around the fishbowl and notice how the color of the "sky" changes as the light reaching your eyes shines across greater and lesser distances through the water. Try positioning the flashlight closer and farther away from the goldfish bowl. Repeat the experiment by adding lesser and greater amounts of milk to the water.

Clouds That Shine in the Night

Sometimes sunset does not bring an abrupt end to the colorful display in the sky. Have you ever heard of noctilucent clouds, meaning "clouds that shine in the night"? These mysterious clouds are not common, and they occur only between about 45 degrees and 80 degrees north and south latitude. In the Northern Hemisphere, that is between Portland, Oregon, and the northern tip of Greenland. You are most likely to see these night-shining clouds low in the western sky between May and mid-August.

People who have seen them say that their upper regions shine with a dazzling silvery blue light and look like the waves of a ghostly ocean with crests dozens of miles apart and troughs several miles deep. Sometimes the clouds appear motionless. Other times they may be speeded along by winds blowing more than 400 miles an hour. Their regions close to the horizon shine a golden yellow.

Most of our weather clouds drift along at a height between about 1,000 feet and 10,000 feet. Noctilucent clouds form at great heights, about 250,000 feet (50 miles) above the surface. That makes them the highest clouds of our planet, riding above more than 99.9 percent of Earth's atmosphere. The clouds usually are visible low in the sky, forming a band between 10 degrees and 20 degrees above the horizon. They begin to appear about fifteen minutes after sunset and are best seen about an hour or more after sunset. Usually they are so thin that the stars can be seen through them. Because Earth's rotation leaves the Sun lower and lower below the western horizon as night wears on, the area of sky lighted by noctilucent clouds narrows with the night.

The fact that the upper parts of the clouds shine with a bluish light suggests that the clouds are made up of very fine particles, which scatter blue light best. It now seems that they are made up of fine, ice-coated particles of dust from meteors and comets, which catch and reflect the Sun's light. An average of 10 tons of this cosmic dust rains down on Earth each day. Right after a cometlike object crashed to earth in Siberia in the year 1908, there were striking displays of noctilucent clouds.

If you view the clouds through binoculars or a small telescope, you will see them better. Binoculars, for instance, will block out the stray light of twilight and bring out the wavy nature of the clouds. For some reason, the clouds seem brighter if you look at them upside down. You can do this by lying down on your back with your head toward the west. This illusion even can be seen by looking at a photograph of noctilucent clouds.

Clouds with Silver Linings

What are clouds? When you are out in the fog, you are standing in a cloud. On a cold winter morning, you see your warm and moist breath as your own private cloud. The jet trails of high-flying aircraft are clouds, and you probably have seen little clouds forming at the ends of automobile exhaust pipes on a cold winter morning. Clouds are made of moisture, or water vapor, that forms small droplets of water around tiny particles of salt and dust in the air.

Those clouds that form about 10,000 feet or higher and that are made up of tiny ice crystals are called cirrus clouds. They usually are so thin that the Sun shines right through them. Clouds lower down are made up of billions of tiny droplets of water. When the droplets are very small, they are light enough to be buoyed up by the air. But if they grow larger, they become heavy enough to fall out of the cloud as rain. Or, in winter, they form delicate ice crystals and fall out of the cold as snow.

Why are clouds white? Since the sky is blue, why aren't clouds blue, also, or green or red or purple? If you take up cloud watching, you will find that sometimes clouds are those other colors.

With the Sun behind you on a warm summer day, you can see fluffy, fair-weather clouds glistening white and looking soft but "solid" enough to stretch out on and take a nap. The water drop-

Clouds can be "seeded" to produce rain or snow, as discovered by Vincent J. Schaefer of the General Electric Laboratory. He breathed into a "cold box" and created a cloud, then waved a cold rod through the cloud, changing water droplets into snow crystals and creating a miniature snowstorm.

lets in these clouds are just the right size to scatter all the wavelengths of sunlight, and that is why these clouds appear white. The next time you are cloud watching, notice what happens to a fluffy white cloud when the Sun passes behind it. The cloud appears to darken except around its thin edges where the Sun is able to shine through. This is the cloud's "silver lining."

In storm clouds, the droplets are larger and block out more of the Sun's rays from reaching us. Another reason storm clouds appear dark is that their larger droplets scatter less light.

Fair weather clouds, like these cumulus clouds, occur between 1,000 and 10,000 feet. They are made up of tiny water droplets formed around tiny grains of dust or salt. When behind such a cloud, the Sun brightens the cloud's edges and so gives the cloud a "silver lining."

Mother-of-pearl Clouds

These luminous clouds are about as rare as noctilucent clouds. Made of tiny ice crystals, they form about 16 miles above the ground, which makes them twice as high as the highest ordinary clouds, but they are far below the noctilucent clouds.

Mother-of-pearl clouds are especially beautiful when seen a bit to the left or right of the setting Sun. Sometimes they are seen in broad banks, shining with the brilliance and rich colors of fish scales. An entire cloud bank may appear almost a single color, while the edges may glisten with all the colors of the rainbow. This effect seems to be caused by the clouds' being made up of ice crystals rather than water droplets. Sometimes the colors change as the Sun sinks lower over the horizon. During the time the Sun is setting, which takes about four minutes, the mother-of-pearl clouds darken.

You are most likely to see mother-of-pearl clouds at sunset just after a storm has swept the air clean. Just before a storm, high-flying cirrus clouds sometimes also are seen to glisten colorfully at sunset. One of the most spectacular sightings of mother-of-pearl clouds took place in mid-May 1910. At that time, Earth passed through the dust tail of Halley's Comet. Possibly the comet dust mixing with these high-altitude clouds caused the unusually spectacular view of them.

5
THE NORTHERN LIGHTS

Those who have seen a truly spectacular display of the Northern Lights say that it is a sight that will live in their memories always. To capture the beauty of the painted night sky in words is impossible. As it shimmers and flames, it may cover nearly half of the northern sky from east to west.

The lights may appear dimly at dusk and then for several hours blend into different glowing colors and weave graceful forms. When they first appear, they may color the graying sky with a yellowish or greenish white light in the form of a great arc. Sometimes for a few hours an arc changes little, slowly falling off toward the south. Then quite suddenly the lower edge grows intense and sharp, and the arc separates into fanlike rays that blaze into pink, purple, and red. Parts of it may take on the form of pastel cosmic draperies—quivering, folding, and unfolding. This part of the show, when the lights fill the entire northern sky, is the climax, but lasts only a few minutes. Gradually the forms dissolve, the intense colors fade, and the sky is left with a faint, glowing light.

The Northern Lights also are called the northern dawn and aurora borealis. There are many different kinds of displays. From my home in the mountains of Rangeley, Maine, I once saw an auroral display end with huge, ghostly, cloudlike patches rapidly flashing brighter and fainter and lighting up the landscape enough for me to see camps on the opposite shore of my lake, a distance of about a mile. The flashing part of the display lasted for about an hour.

If you ever see an especially good auroral display, you may feel as I have felt—each moment waiting for a cosmic rumbling sound of some sort. But all auroras are silent, for they occur 100 or so miles above the ground. At that height, the air is nearly a perfect vacuum and so cannot carry sound.

Although the Northern Lights may be seen now and then throughout the year, they are especially bright and frequent when there is lots of activity on the Sun, which happens in cycles of eleven years. The last period of activity was around 1979, so the next period should be around 1990.

To understand what causes auroras, we must know something about "storms" on the Sun and about the way Earth acts as a giant magnet.

Storms on the Sun

The Sun is a huge ball of extremely hot gases, mostly hydrogen along with some helium and small amounts of other elements. The gaseous surface of the Sun has a temperature of about 6,000° Celsius. That is hot enough to break apart the hydrogen and helium atoms. So, instead of whole atoms on the Sun, there are electrically charged bits and pieces of atoms. These pieces are in the form of tiny particles called electrons and protons.

Whenever the Sun is especially active, very hot gases from deep beneath its fiery surface well up and leap hundreds of thousands of miles into the sky. In the form of gigantic spikes or enormous fiery loops, they may tumble back to the surface or escape off into space. Other outbursts form hot, gaseous geysers that leap skyward at speeds of several hundred miles a second and reach heights of more than 50,000 miles.

And try to imagine a lake of gasoline into which someone drops a lighted match. Such flash explosions—but of gases, not of gasoline—occur in the Sun's lower atmosphere and are called flares. They range in size from a few miles to several thousand miles, and their explosive violence lasts anywhere from a few minutes to an hour or so. A single flare may release the energy of 10 million hydrogen bombs and reach temperatures greater than 20 million degrees. At times of peak activity, there is at least one flare every hour or so. All of these solar storms cast off streams of electrons and protons that race across space and batter Earth's upper atmosphere. We call the streams of charged particles blowing out from the Sun the solar wind.

Earth as a Magnet

Our planet is a giant magnet. Like a simple bar magnet, it has north and south magnetic poles that make compass needles point the way they do. Magnetic lines of force form a magnetic field that loops out of the magnetic north pole down to the magnetic south pole. The entire magnetic force field is called the magnetosphere. It is squashed up on the side of our planet facing the Sun and stretched out into a long tail on the opposite side by the solar wind.

The magnetosphere has two huge, doughnut-shaped rings called the Van Allen radiation belts. Most of the dangerous charged particles of the solar wind are detoured around Earth by the magnetic field and so we are protected from their harmful radiation effects. But some of these particles are trapped temporarily in the Van Allen belts.

Planet Earth is a gigantic magnet with a force field looping out around it as if a huge bar magnet were stuck inside the planet and reaching from north to south. Notice that Earth has two north poles—a geographic north pole and a magnetic north pole—and that they are not aligned.

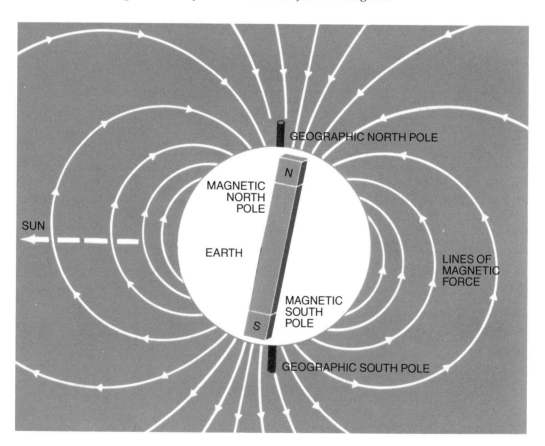

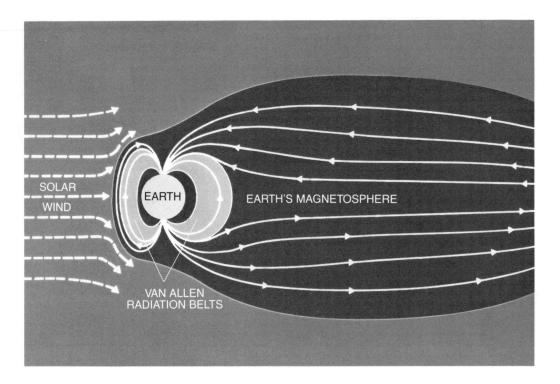

Earth's magnetic field gets squashed up by the solar wind on the Sun-facing side but is stretched out on the opposite side. Two doughnut-shaped zones of magnetism, called the Van Allen belts, deflect the solar wind. Other planets in the Solar System have similar properties.

What Causes Auroras?

The colorful displays of Northern Lights are turned on when solar wind particles are first caught up in the magnetic field, then speeded up by the Van Allen belts, and finally hurled into Earth's upper atmosphere where they collide with atoms and molecules formed mostly of oxygen and nitrogen. Each time an oxygen or nitrogen atom is struck, it loses one or more electrons. But almost immediately it finds one or more loose electrons and replaces the

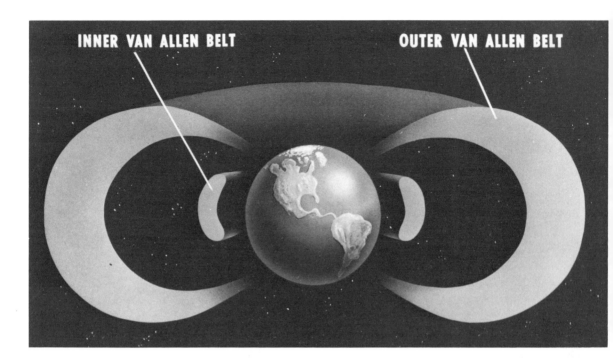

INNER VAN ALLEN BELT   OUTER VAN ALLEN BELT

The Van Allen radiation belts are huge doughnut-shaped rings of radiation particles trapped from the solar wind. When these particles are speeded up by the Van Allen belts and hurled into Earth's upper air, we see the colorful displays of Northern Lights.

lost one. As it does, the atom gives off a little burst of energy that we see as light.

When oxygen atoms regain lost electrons, they give off bursts of green or red light. So it is the energy bursts of oxygen atoms that account for the green, pink, and reddish colors of an auroral display. When nitrogen molecules regain lost electrons, they give off bursts of violet or blue light. The green light coming from the activity of oxygen, and the violet light from nitrogen molecules, occur about 70 miles above Earth's surface. We see the bursts of reddish light from oxygen atoms from 125 to 250 miles high.

Different Colors at Different Heights

Three or four times every ten years or so, a beautiful aurora that glows a rosy red appears at a height of 185 to 250 miles. Gales of protons sweeping into the upper atmosphere often cause a faint, luminous band of greenish white light. A few hours after a flare erupts on the Sun, streams of high-speed protons excite the upper air and produce a greenish white "polar-cap glow."

High-altitude nuclear-bomb tests have produced bright and deep red auroras. They have produced other effects as well. A notable test that took place on July 8, 1962, turned out street lights in Hawaii, some 800 miles away, raised havoc with burglar alarms and circuit breakers, and shortened the useful lives of several artificial satellites!

One of the most spectacular auroras ever reported took place on the night of February 11, 1958, following a strong solar flare two days earlier. A band of colorful lights 1,250 miles wide circled the Arctic like a gigantic headband and dipped down over North America. The band looped eastward from Redmond, Oregon, across to Hanover, New Hampshire.

6
HALOS, SUNDOGS, AND ARCS

Chances are that most of you have seen a ring around the Sun or around the Moon. But chances are just as good that you have not taken the time to appreciate these halos in the sky. They appear in many forms and are grand sights, especially when seen in splendid color at sunset or sunrise.

We usually can see Sun or Moon halos when the weather changes before a storm. At such times, high, thin cirrus clouds move in at heights of 30,000 to 50,000 feet. Since the temperature is well below freezing at those heights, water vapor in the air quickly freezes and forms different shapes of tiny ice crystals. Halos are best seen when the cirrus clouds are spread thinly and evenly so that a ghostly Sun or Moon can shine through them. These are called cirrostratus clouds. Halos are common in April and May in regions where the weather changes often, but they are visible at other times of the year as well. People who make a habit

46

A ring around the Sun, or Sun halo, sometimes can be seen in splendid color around sunrise or sunset. You can safely observe one by keeping the Sun behind a tree or a house and looking at the resulting half halo. The most common Sun halo is the 22-degree halo, like this one.

of studying the sky for pleasure report that from 100 to 200 halos can be seen in one year. Sun halos appear more often than Moon halos, and they are brighter and more colorful. Along with Sun halos we can also see several other kinds of arcs and circles.

Small-Ring and Big-Ring Halos

The most common Sun halo is the 22-degree halo. It is called that because of its size. The distance from the center of the Sun to the inner edge of the halo is 22 degrees—or two fists wide, if you measure by holding your fists together at arm's length with the thumbs against each other. So the complete distance across the halo from inner edge to the opposite inner edge is four fists. The first time you see a 22-degree halo, it may seem enormous, but this is a small-ring halo. Sometimes there are large-ring (46-degree) halos.

A good way—and a safe way—to observe a Sun halo is from the shade of a house or a tree. By keeping the Sun behind the tree, you can still see nearly half of the halo. *Never* look directly at the Sun, not even through a veil of cirrus clouds. Doing so can permanently damage your eyes. You can measure Sun—and Moon—halos with the measuring device described below.

HOW TO MEASURE HALOS IN THE SKY

Here is a way you can measure angles up and down or back and forth across the sky.

Cut a long, thin piece of wood into two pieces—one 3 feet long and the other about 4 feet long. Now you will need someone to help you. Sit down on the ground, hold the 3-foot-long stick under

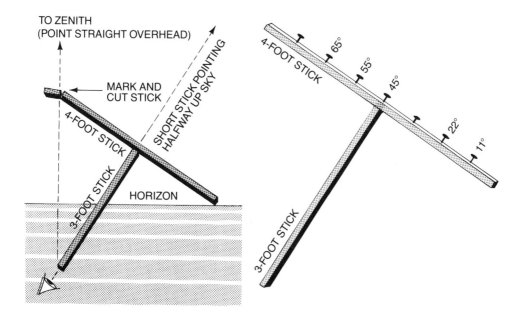

By arranging two lengths of wood in the shape of a T and marking the cross piece so that angular distance can be measured (as explained in the text), you can measure the height of an object above the horizon or the width of a Sun or Moon halo, for example.

your eye, and aim it halfway up the sky as exactly as you can. Then have your helper hold the other piece across the end to form a T, with the top of the T (your helper's stick) pointing up and down, *not* level with the horizon. The bottom end of your helper's stick should appear exactly on the distant flat horizon.

Next, have your helper make a mark near the top end of his or her stick. That mark should appear to you to be exactly overhead. Cut the stick to the length marked by your helper and then attach the two pieces of wood to make the T. Make sure that you attach the 3-foot-long piece exactly halfway along the other piece. Now double-check by aiming your angle measurer halfway up the sky and making sure one end rests on the horizon and the opposite end is at the very top of the sky exactly overhead.

Drive a tack or small nail into the T-stick where the 3-foot stick is attached, as shown in the diagram. With a felt pen, mark that position 45 degrees. Now measure halfway between the nail and each end of the T-bar. Drive a tack into each of those points and mark one of them 22 degrees and the other 65 degrees. If you want to, you can measure halfway between the T-bar end and the 22-degree tack and mark that spot 11 degrees. You can also mark a 55-degree spot halfway between the 45-degree and 65-degree tacks. You now have a fairly accurate way of measuring what astronomers call angular distance up and down or across the sky. You can use your angle measurer to measure the height of a star above the horizon, the width of a halo, or the height of a rainbow.

A Sun halo is produced by the reflection and bending of light, similar to the way a rainbow is produced. But in the case of halos, ice crystals — not water droplets — do the reflecting and bending. Sometimes halos are a pale white, which usually happens when the cirrus clouds are uneven. Other times they are brightly colored. The colors are best when the clouds form an even haze instead of being uneven. The inner edge of a halo will be red and fairly sharp. Outside the red band will be other bands, sometimes of yellow, green, white, and blue. The yellow, however, may not be very noticeable.

Ideally, the color range and brightness of each band from red to violet in a Sun halo *should* be like a rainbow, but that is rarely the case. The reason is that in a Sun halo ice crystals—not smoothly shaped water droplets—are refracting the light. The shape of the crystals, their size, and how they are arranged in space beside each other all help determine the colorfulness and the size of a Sun halo.

But nearly always we can expect a sharp red inner edge because the red wavelengths are bent least and, therefore, come through brighter. A greater bending of the shorter wavelengths by the haphazardly arranged ice crystals results in not only weaker, washed-out colors, but a blending of colors on the orange side of red.

The next time you see a Sun halo, notice that the sky inside the halo is darker than the sky outside it. This is because the inner rim of red light is scattered less and refracted less than the outer rim of blue. The greater scattering and bending of blue light causes the blue rim to be fuzzy and the sky beyond it to be lighter. That also is why the sky is darker between the two bands of a double rainbow than it is on either side of the rainbows. As with a double rainbow, sometimes you can see a second and fainter halo. The outer one is called the 46-degree halo, because of its larger size, but 46-degree halos may sometimes be seen by themselves, although they are rare.

Moon halos also are common. They are caused by the same play of reflecting and bending of light that causes Sun halos, but Moon halos are fainter and less colorful. Both Moon and Sun halos often are signs of rainy weather on the way. This is because the appearance of high cirrus clouds that cause the halos are early indications that a low-pressure weather system is moving in.

Ice Crystals—Bullets, Plates, and Columns

The ice crystals that cause Sun and Moon halos come in different shapes and sizes. As those shapes and sizes differ, so do the halos, arcs, and other displays they cause. The shape an ice crystal takes depends mostly on the temperature of the cloud. There are five

Rings around the Moon are common but less colorful than Sun halos. Both Moon and Sun halos are caused by high cirrus clouds of ice crystals that reflect and refract light from the Moon or Sun. The inner edge of these halos is red, the color brightness depending on the nature of the crystals.

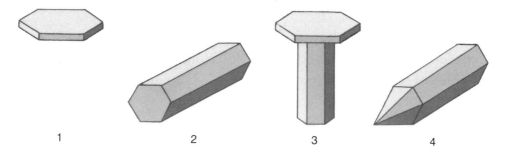

There are several basic shapes of ice crystals. They include (1) plates, (2) columns, (3) capped columns, and (4) bullets. Still others have the varied shapes of snowflakes. The particular shapes and sizes of ice crystals determine the quality of a halo, arc, or other display.

basic shapes, but each shape comes in several different sizes: (1) Some ice crystals, called plates, are flat, six-sided discs shaped like a bathroom floor tile. They form when the cloud temperature is − 12°C. (2) Those called columns are shaped like a short section of a six-sided pencil and form at about − 5°C. (3) Others, called capped columns, are shaped like a column with a plate on top. (4) Those called bullets have the shape of a column with a point at one end. They form at − 20°C. (5) And still others, which form at about − 15°C, have the many shapes of snowflakes.

Sunlight or moonlight shining through these differently shaped ice crystals gets reflected and refracted, just as sunlight does when it enters a water droplet of a rainbow. The effect in both cases is the same—some of the white light is broken down into its series of rainbow colors with red at one end and blue-violet at the other.

Sometimes a cloud contains mostly crystals of one type all neatly positioned the same way, like soldiers on parade. Sometimes there is a mixture of crystals of different types and different sizes. When the crystals are tiny, molecules of the air juggle them about. As the crystals grow larger they tumble down, spinning as they fall and

bumping the air molecules out of the way. All of these things—
position, size, shape, and motion of cloud crystals—determine
which of the many different kinds of halos you may see.

Sundogs, Arcs, and Pillars

The 22-degree halo is made by small crystals positioned every
which way. Very small crystals cause a whitish halo with a red
edge. Sometimes an ice-crystal cloud is made up mostly of bullets,
plates, and capped columns, all about medium size and neatly

In days of old, people feared the strange sights in the sky caused by atmo-
spheric conditions. Such appearances included mock Suns, or "sundogs,"
as shown in this woodcut done in 1563.

arranged upright as they gently fall from the cloud. I have several times flown through a brigade of such crystals, all glittering like miniature diamonds in the sunlight. They are much smaller than snowflakes and should not be confused with them, or with sleet. A cloud spawning such crystals produces a 22-degree halo along with certain patches and arcs of light. The patches are called sundogs or mock Suns or parhelia.

When sundogs appear, usually there are two—one on either side of the halo and the same height as the Sun. When the Sun is on the horizon, the sundogs appear on the rim of the halo. The higher the Sun is in the sky, the farther out from the halo the sundogs will appear. When the Sun is 50 degrees above the horizon, the sundogs will be 10 degrees away from the halo. Sometimes only one sundog is visible, and sometimes one or both will be visible, but the halo will not be.

Sundogs usually are brighter than the halo and may be dazzling. They are clearly red on the inside, with a middle band of yellow that changes to a bluish white part slightly stretched out into a tail that points away from the Sun. The tails are best seen when the Sun is low. As the crystals causing the sundogs gently fall, they wobble a bit. It is this wobbling motion that makes sundogs appear as fuzzy patches rather than with the sharp edge of a rainbow. Once in a great while, you may see sundogs with a second set of sundogs attached. It is not certain whether 46-degree halos have sundogs. Reports of them are rare.

An especially beautiful member of the halo family is one formed by bullets and capped columns. It is a brightly colored short curve, or arc, very nearly straight overhead next to the zenith position, which is the straight overhead point in the sky. Called the circumzenith arc (meaning "arc around the zenith"), it is not often observed by most people because so few of us ever look straight up. This lovely arc is visible only when the Sun is less than about 32 degrees above the horizon. When the Sun is at 32 degrees, the arc appears as a patch, but as the Sun lowers, the patch opens into an arc of color. Since arcs appear quite a distance above the Sun, there is no danger in observing them.

In 1821, the British explorer Sir William E. Parry reported seeing a 22-degree halo with a small arc just above it and another just below. Called Parry arcs, these change shape and color as the Sun moves up or down the sky. They are caused by column ice crystals falling flat on their sides instead of straight up and down.

Fairly often, you can see a delicate feather of light reaching upward from the rising or setting sun. Called a solar pillar, it is best seen by blocking out the Sun, either with your hand or by viewing from the shadow of a house or tree. Sometimes a pillar may be tilted slightly or be seen below the Sun. Pillars are caused by capped columns and plates. When seen at sunrise or sunset, they take on the Sun's color, so they may be orange or red. Pillars, like sundogs, appear fuzzy because the ice crystals causing them wobble as they drift down through the air. In winter, if there is fog made of ice crystals, you may see pillars on top of street lamps and airport runway lights at night.

Once in a while, you can see a 22-degree halo, sundogs, and a pillar all at once, and the combination may form crosses in the sky. Could this display be what caused people of long ago to link halos with heaven? One of the best-known accounts of ice-crystal crosses in the sky took place in the summer of 1865. Edward Whymper and his mountain-climbing party had just become the first to reach the top of the famous Matterhorn mountain on the border of Italy and Switzerland. On their way down, four of the climbers fell to their deaths. Later that day, Whymper saw the display just described, only there were three crosses. He later said that he had never seen such a display, and for the crosses to have appeared at that particular time seemed strange to him.

This photograph shows a single sundog as a thin tail pointing to the right away from the Sun. Called parhelia, these displays are caused by ice-crystal clouds between us and the Sun.

7
GHOSTLY LIGHT
OF THE ZODIAC

As the last colors of evening twilight fade and the darkness of the winter sky deepens, a soft patch of light shaped like a gigantic gumdrop appears low in the western sky. Called the Zodiacal light, it has been known and puzzled over for hundreds of years. It is best seen from positions along Earth's equator but also is visible from midnorthern and midsouthern latitudes, where it shines more faintly.

A Light from the Past

The Zodiacal light is not given off by the Zodiac but appears along that imaginary belt of constellations. No one knows who first recognized the pattern of constellations forming the Zodiac. We can picture the Zodiac as an imaginary highway 16 degrees wide forming a complete circle of 360 degrees around the sky.

The Zodiac is a belt of twelve constellations that form a band around the sky, following the apparent path traced by the Sun throughout a year. The constellations are Pisces, Aries, Taurus, Gemini, Cancer, Leo, Virgo, Libra, Scorpio, Sagittarius, Capricorn, and Aquarius.

Apollo astronauts while in orbit around the Moon took this photograph of the Zodiacal light. It was taken just after the Sun set below the edge of the Moon.

Appearing along this highway at regular intervals are the twelve constellations that make up the Zodiac: Aries, the Ram; Taurus, the Bull; Gemini, the Twins; Cancer, the Crab; Leo, the Lion; Virgo, the Virgin; Libra, the Scales; Scorpio, the Scorpion; Sagittarius, the Archer; Capricorn, the Sea-goat; Aquarius, the Water-carrier; and Pisces, the Fishes. The Sun and its nine planets all are seen to travel along this highway of the sky month by month throughout the year, the Sun completing one trip around the Zodiac every 365 days.

The Zodiacal light appears as a glowing mist that stretches along the Zodiac something like the faint glow of the Milky Way but more foglike. The light is brightest and broadest close to the Sun, which means that we see it best soon after sunset and soon before sunrise.

About two hours after sunset, the Sun is 18 degrees below the horizon. When conditions are right, you will see a broad and fuzzy cone of dim light rising in the Zodiac in the southwest. By the time the Sun reaches 20 degrees below the horizon, the sky is darker and the Zodiacal light takes the shape of an enormous faint pyramid with rounded edges reaching up from the horizon. It is brightest down near the horizon where it is closest to the Sun. By an hour or two before midnight, this west Zodiacal light almost fades from view. But if you look in the east an hour or two after midnight, you will see a faint glow of the east Zodiacal light. Earth's rotation has brought the Sun around so that we are now viewing the early-morning sky. As the Sun continues its apparent climb up toward the eastern horizon, the east Zodiacal light fills a larger region of sky and becomes brighter. It is brightest about an hour before sunrise, just before the first glow of dawn begins to mask it from view.

Although they are not as easy to find as Sun halos, an experienced sky watcher usually can find both the evening and dawn Zodiacal light from October through March. The best view is the evening glow during January, February, and March, but in late spring the light of the Milky Way becomes bothersome. The second best is the morning glow during October, November, and December.

If the Moon is out, or there are lights around you, don't waste your time searching. The sky must be dark. Even the light of the bright planets Venus or Jupiter can cause trouble. Being high on a hilltop with a clear view of a dark sky all around you is ideal.

What Causes the Light?

For hundreds of years, scientists thought that the Zodiacal light was sunlight scattered high in the atmosphere long after sunset. Today we know that that cannot be so. The Zodiacal light is about the same color as sunlight—whitish. If the light were scattered by air molecules high in the atmosphere, the result would be a blue glow, not a white one. That is so because particles the size of air molecules scatter blue light best. Larger particles are needed to account for the scattering of white light.

Nearly 300 years ago, the European astronomer J. D. Cassini studied the Zodiacal light for about ten years. He thought that a thinly spread cloud of dust out among the planets reflected sunlight and so accounted for what we see. The effect would be the same as viewing a streetlight at night through a heavy fog, when the light is surrounded by a glowing haze. The fact that there are an east and a west Zodiacal light made Cassini suppose that his dust cloud was spread out all around the Sun. There matters stood for many years.

Later, scientists suspected that the Sun's extremely thin outer atmosphere, the corona, might cause the Zodiacal glow. But studies have shown that there are too few particles (electrons) in the corona to reflect light as bright as the Zodiacal light.

It turns out that Cassini was right after all. Astronomers pretty much agree now that a disc-shaped cloud of matter is spread out around the Sun, matter left over from the time the planets were formed some 4.6 billion years ago. The matter consists of particles ranging in size from dust grains to tiny asteroids up to 3 feet or so across. This cloud of matter seems to be denser near the Sun and then thins out beyond the orbit of Mars. Such a cloud of matter made up of particles much larger than air molecules would scatter sunlight and account for the color and brightness of the Zodiacal light. Because the cloud is denser near the Sun and thinner out near Mars, an astronaut on Mercury would see the Zodiacal light as a bright band all across the sky. An astronaut on Mars would see the Sun as we see our streetlight through a heavy fog.

Searching for the Gegenschein

When you are watching the Zodiacal light an hour or so before midnight, look near the zenith and see if you can see a patch of very dim light. The extremely faint glow would form a bridge linking the east and west Zodiacal lights, if you saw them both at the same time. This faint glow is called the gegenschein (meaning "counter-glow"). It was given that name because it appears exactly opposite the Sun's position. So, if you see the gegenschein exactly overhead at the zenith, you know that the Sun is exactly underfoot at the opposite side of Earth.

The gegenschein was first described by the German astronomer T. J. C. A. Brorsen in 1854. Without doubt, it is the hardest of all sky events to find. Seeing it requires the blackest of nights away from city lights and with no Moon or nearby glow of the Milky Way.

As with the Zodiacal light, the cause of the gegenschein was not discovered until this century. Some thought that the glow was from a part of Earth's upper atmosphere pushed out into a gas tail by the solar wind. The tail was said to be about 800,000 miles out in space. This idea died when someone pointed out that a glowing cloud at that distance from Earth, and opposite the Sun, would have a dark spot on it. The spot would be Earth's shadow.

The gegenschein is caused by the reflection of sunlight from the same disc-shaped cloud of matter left over from the time the planets were formed. The effect is the same as when the Sun, on the opposite side of Earth from the Moon, lights up the Moon's entire face and we see the full Moon. In the same way, the Sun is lighting up billions upon billions of those Zodiacal-light particles lying directly along a line formed by the alignment of the Sun and Earth. The reason that there is no shadow-spot in the middle of the gegenschein cloud is that the glow lies beyond the distance where Earth would cast a shadow.

Again, don't be disappointed if you can't find the gegenschein. Many astronomers and experienced sky watchers have never seen this patch of pale light.

8
ECLIPSES AND STAR TRAILS

An eclipse is a lovely sight and can be a thrilling experience if you know how to look and what to look for. Because of the way the Moon moves around Earth, and the way Earth moves around the Sun, the total number of eclipses in a year changes. There can be as many as seven—four or five eclipses of the Sun and two or three of the Moon. Or there can be as few as two eclipses a year, both of the Sun. The only way you could see every eclipse would be to travel to that part of the world where each eclipse is visible.

Watching Lunar Eclipses

As the Sun shines and lights up Earth, Earth forms a cone-shaped shadow 856,000 miles long off into space. Ordinarily, we are not aware of that shadow because we cannot see it. Sometimes, however, we do become aware of it. As the Moon circles Earth, once in

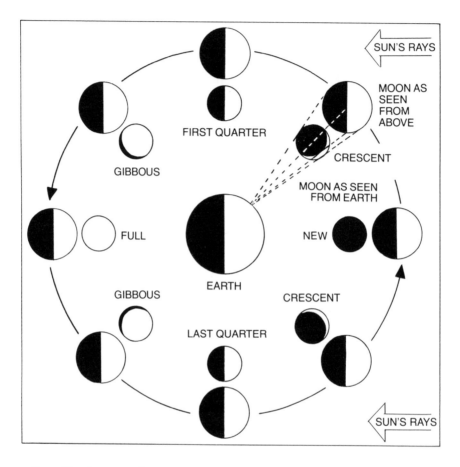

SUN'S RAYS

MOON AS SEEN FROM ABOVE

FIRST QUARTER

GIBBOUS

CRESCENT

MOON AS SEEN FROM EARTH

FULL

NEW

EARTH

GIBBOUS

CRESCENT

LAST QUARTER

SUN'S RAYS

From Earth we see the Moon go through phases. But if you were in space above Earth's North Pole, the Moon would always appear to be half full, as would Earth.

a while it glides through Earth's shadow and we see an eclipse of the Moon, called a lunar eclipse.

A lunar eclipse can take place only when the Moon is on one side of Earth and the Sun is on the opposite side. Once every month, at full Moon, the Sun, Earth, and Moon are lined up that way. Then, why don't we see a lunar eclipse once a month at every full Moon? The reason is that the Moon circles Earth on a tilt that sometimes takes the Moon above Earth's shadow and sometimes below it. At such times, we see a full Moon and not an eclipse. The diagram on the opposite page shows how different phases of the Moon occur. When the Moon passes partly through Earth's shadow, we see a partial lunar eclipse. It is only when the Moon passes completely through Earth's shadow that we see a total lunar eclipse. Because Earth's shadow is so much larger than the Moon, a total lunar eclipse can last as long as two hours.

As the Moon moves across Earth's shadow during a total lunar eclipse, it passes through two different shadow zones. There is a

An eclipse of the Moon, called a lunar eclipse, occurs when the Sun, Earth, and the Moon are aligned so that the Moon passes through Earth's shadow as it orbits Earth. There are two shadow zones—a lighter one, the penumbra; and a darker one, the umbra.

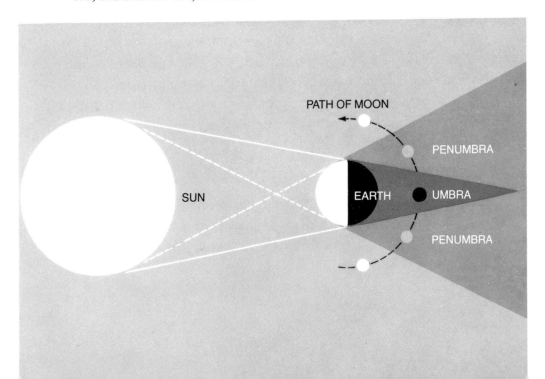

deep, central shadow, called the umbra, and a second shadow zone around the umbra, called the penumbra. The penumbra is not as dark a shadow zone as the umbra. So, during a total lunar eclipse, the Moon first enters the penumbra and darkens a bit. It next enters the umbra and grows still darker. It then passes through the umbra and out into the opposite side of the penumbra and lightens a bit. And finally it leaves the penumbra and again appears bright and full.

There are three different types of lunar eclipses: (1) We see a penumbral eclipse when the Moon passes through the penumbra shadow but misses the umbra. (2) We see a partial lunar eclipse when the Moon passes through the penumbra but only partly through the umbra. (3) We see a total lunar eclipse when the Moon passes completely through the umbra.

No two lunar eclipses are exactly the same. And it is rare when the Moon fades completely from sight during an eclipse. Even when the Moon is in the middle of the umbra, we can usually see it shining softly with a faint copper red glow surrounded by brighter colors. The outer edge may appear as a rim of delicate pink. Moving inward, the colors change to a pale gold, then to a sea green. We also can make out the major features of the Moon, such as the outlines of the great, dark areas called maria, meaning "seas."

Since the Moon is completely in Earth's shadow during a total eclipse, what causes it to shine? The answer is Earth's atmosphere.

What Causes Moonshine?

As sunlight passes through Earth's atmosphere, the air acts as a prism and refracts some of the light into the shadow zone so that it falls on the eclipsed Moon. As the diagram shows, rays passing

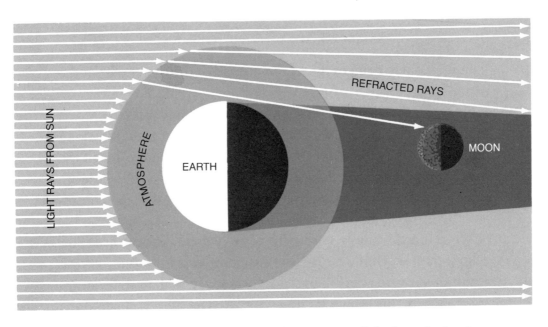

We see the Moon during mid-eclipse because some light from the Sun is refracted by Earth's atmosphere in such a way that it is bent in and dimly lights the Moon's surface. At such times, we may see the Moon bathed in a dull reddish light. The color changes as the Moon moves into the penumbra.

through the deep, dense air layers near Earth's surface are bent more than the rays that pass through the thin upper air, And on passing through the denser parts of the air, some of the light is lost to sight due to scattering. This is true for the blue and violet rays. The orange and red rays are scattered least and so make up most of the light that is bent into the shadow zone and illuminates the eclipsed Moon. That is what accounts for the copper red glow of the Moon during mideclipse.

The rim of lighter colors is caused by sunlight passing through Earth's thin upper air layers. Less of that light is lost by scattering, so some of the blue and green rays get through. And because these are refracted less sharply than the orange and red rays, they also light up the outer rim of the Moon instead of the center part of the Moon's face.

Since it is light shining through Earth's air that causes the Moon to glow during an eclipse, changes in the clearness or amount of pollution in the air should change the brightness and color of the Moon glow from one eclipse to the next. And so it does. There are bright and colorful lunar eclipses, there are dark, colorless eclipses, and there are others at every stage in between.

When Earth's air is especially dirty, we can expect a darker eclipse than when the air is clean. A major volcanic eruption or a major dust storm sometimes sends dust or ash high into the atmosphere where it is blown far and wide. At such times, much of the sunlight refracted into the shadow zone is scattered and lost. That is when we see dark lunar eclipses. At other times, a certain amount of dust particles in the air can scatter the blue and violet rays almost completely so that only yellow, orange, and red rays reach the shadow zone. Then we see an especially reddish eclipsed Moon, perhaps with a yellowish rim.

HOW TO PHOTOGRAPH A LUNAR ECLIPSE

You don't have to be afraid of damaging your eyes by watching a lunar eclipse. Watching a lunar eclipse is no more dangerous than looking at the Moon at any other time. That also means that it's safe to watch a lunar eclipse through a telescope or through a camera lens.

You don't need expensive gadgets to get excellent photos of the next eclipse. All you need is a tripod and a camera that can take time exposures. And be sure to use color film with a speed of ASA 400, which will be printed on the film box. Also make sure that the film is not old and beyond its useful date, which also is printed on the box.

If you have a standard lens of about 50mm, you will not be able to get a very big image of the Moon on the film. It will be only a small fraction of an inch across (1mm). But don't worry, you can still get a splendid photo. Here's what to do:

Well before the eclipse, watch the Moon to find out in what direction it is moving across the sky. Then be ready to set your camera and tripod so that at the moment the eclipse begins the image of the Moon will be at the *edge* of your viewfinder, *not* in the middle. What you are going to do is to take a series of exposures all on one frame. You should end up with a train of exposures.

To take this photo, make sure that your tripod is positioned the way you want it to be and that it is locked firmly so that it won't move during the series of exposures. Set the lens at f5.6 and make your first exposure of the full and bright Moon at 1/2000 second. Do *not* advance the film, because you will be making a series of "double exposures," actually multiple exposures. Make other exposures as follows:

Moon's Position	Exposure Time
Full (uneclipsed) Moon	1/2000 sec.
Moon deep within penumbra	1/1000
Part of Moon in penumbra	1/125
Part of Moon in umbra	1/4
Moon just within umbra	1
Moon centered in umbra	4

Notice that the exposures become longer as the eclipse progresses. This is necessary because the Moon darkens steadily as the eclipse proceeds toward totality. So exposure times must become longer in order to catch the Moon's dimming light.

You should plan ahead for this rare event. The newspapers will tell in advance how long the eclipse will last in your area. A month before the eclipse, have a practice session making exposures of the full Moon at intervals for the length of time the eclipse will take. Then have the film processed so you can see your results. You can, of course, make single-frame exposures throughout the eclipse, snapping off exposures as often as you wish. If someone else photographs along with you, one of you could try the "double exposure" series while the other takes single-frame shots.

To get a large single image of the Moon, you will need at least a 300mm telephoto lens. The more powerful the telephoto lens, the larger the image will be. If you have a telescope, even better. Photographing with a telephoto lens or through the eyepiece of your telescope should produce good single shots. When the Moon is in the penumbral stage, try exposures of 1/500, 1/250, and 1/125 second with ASA 400 film. When the Moon is in the umbral stage, make several exposures ranging from 1/30 second to 10 seconds. Don't be afraid to experiment with different exposure times, which is called "bracketing."

Solar Eclipses

Today it is hard for us to imagine the terror that people of old felt when an eclipse of the Sun took place. The ancient Chinese thought that angry sky dragons were taking bites out of the Sun and devouring it. To frighten the dragons away, warriors beat drums, rattled heavy gongs, shouted, and shot arrows into the air. And apparently they succeeded, since the Sun always reappeared in its full glory.

Even though we know what causes eclipses of the Sun today, experiencing a total solar eclipse can still be very moving. Eclipses of the Sun are much trickier to observe and record than eclipses of the Moon. An eclipse of the Sun takes place when the Moon passes between Earth and the Sun and so blocks out the Sun's light.

An eclipse of the Sun, called a solar eclipse, occurs when the Sun, Earth, and the Moon are aligned so that the Moon's passage between Earth and the Sun casts a shadow-path along part of Earth's surface. Those in the shadow-path see an eclipse; those outside the path do not.

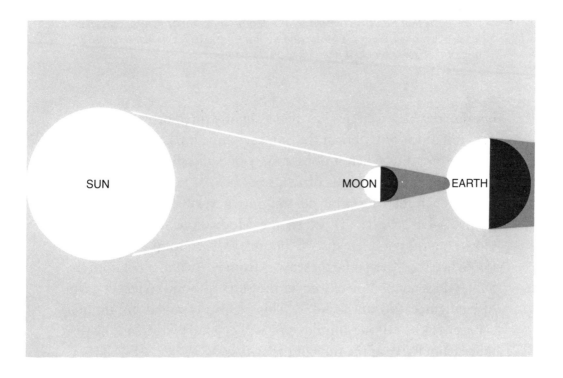

There are three kinds of solar eclipses: a partial eclipse (left) *when only part of the Sun's disc is covered by the Moon; an annular eclipse* (center) *when a rim of sunlight is visible; and a total eclipse* (right) *when the entire disc of the Sun is blocked from view by the Moon.*

Because the Moon circles Earth in a slightly tilted orbit, the Moon does not block our view of the Sun each time it passes between us and the Sun. But when it does, it may do so in three ways and so cause three different kinds of eclipses:

(1) When the Moon blocks out only part of the Sun, we see a partial solar eclipse. (2) When the Moon is nearest Earth and blocks out the complete disc of the Sun, we see a total solar eclipse. (3) When the Moon is farthest away from Earth and blocks out the Sun, it does not completely cover the Sun's disc and so leaves a rim of sunlight called an annulus. This eclipse is called an annular eclipse. The size of the annulus ring will depend on the Moon's distance from Earth at the time of the eclipse.

As the Moon moves along in its orbit during a solar eclipse, and as Earth rotates on its axis, the Moon's cone-shaped shadow traces a path over part of Earth's surface. The path of the annular eclipse of May 30, 1984, moved northeast across Mexico and the Gulf of Mexico, through Louisiana, Mississippi, Georgia, South Carolina, North Carolina, Virginia, and then out to sea. Also, the width of a solar eclipse path changes, depending on the distance of the Moon. In the case of the 1984 eclipse, the path was 17 miles wide in Mexico but narrowed to less than 5 miles over Virginia. Anyone along this eclipse path saw an annular eclipse. Anyone north or south of the path saw only a partial eclipse. People in Alaska were too far north to see any eclipse at all. The last solar eclipse that was seen over such a large part of the United States was in 1979. The next one will be in 1994.

Light and Shadow Effects

Of the three kinds of solar eclipses, the total eclipse is the loveliest. When the Moon is centered on the Sun, the intensely bright ring bursts into a string of bright beads that sparkle like a diamond necklace. The effect lasts from 10 to 20 seconds. The spots of light are called Baily's beads, named after the British astronomer Francis Baily who described them in 1836. This dazzling display during the moments of total eclipse is caused by the Moon's high mountains, which block out some sunlight, and deep valleys, which let some sunlight flash through.

As a total solar eclipse begins, the sky does not darken noticeably. You will not be aware of darkening until about half the Sun's disc is hidden. When about three-quarters of the disc is covered, the part still visible appears darker than before, and reddish. From that point on, the sky darkens quickly. When the Sun is completely hidden, we often have a breathtaking view of the Sun's thin outer atmosphere, the corona, which is spread out around the Sun as a pearly, feathery veil. You may see the corona for a second or so to several minutes. Words cannot describe the beauty of a grand coronal display.

The so-called diamond-ring effect of an annular solar eclipse may be seen at the time of maximum eclipse and lasts about two seconds. It is caused by two or more of Baily's beads forming a cluster of bright light.

During a total eclipse of the Sun, when its disc is completely covered, we get a splendid view of the Sun's thin outer atmosphere, which is called the corona, meaning "crown." A delicate feathery halo, it streams far out into space, crossing Earth's orbit.

Another thing to watch for during a total eclipse of the Sun is how the sky color changes. The half of the sky where the Moon's shadow is, gradually turns a dark purple, as if a storm were on the way. Look around you at all the other parts of the sky and notice color changes. Some parts, outside the corona, sometimes appear a warm orange color.

During a solar eclipse, notice the shadows cast on the ground by the leaves of trees. Sunlight shining down through the small openings between the leaves is projected on the ground in the shape of the Sun at the moment. Before totality, you will see hundreds of tiny crescents shining on the ground. They are large, small, bright, or dim, and all lined up in the same direction. Throughout the eclipse, their shapes keep changing as the shape of the eclipsed Sun continues to change. Hold your hand at different heights above the ground and notice the shadow-shapes of your fingers. They will appear clawlike when the eclipsed Sun is a crescent. If photography is a hobby of yours, you may want to photograph these little Suns among the shadows.

If you happen to be on a farm or other place where there are animals about, watch how they behave at mideclipse when it grows dark. Birds suddenly stop their chirping and begin to settle down for the night. Farm animals huddle together or head for their night shelters. Night creatures, such as bats and owls, emerge from hiding and become active. Horses, mules, and oxen seem to become afraid and often refuse to move. Flowers and other plant parts that usually close at night may close during a long eclipse. But when the Sun comes out again, birds, horses, flowers, and all other day creatures resume their daytime activities. Bats, owls, and other night creatures return to their hiding places and will not reappear until the real night comes.

HOW TO WATCH A SOLAR ECLIPSE—SAFELY

Elsewhere in this book I have warned about *never* looking straight at the Sun, not even for a moment. Long gazes at the Sun will damage your eyes and permanently harm your vision. It is not worth risking even brief looks. Since that is so, then how do you watch an eclipse of the Sun?

The answer is by projection. What does that mean? It means by shining an image of the Sun onto a piece of white cardboard and watching the image instead of the Sun itself. There are several ways of doing this, and they all are safe. One is to punch four or five neat pinholes in a sheet of heavy construction paper or thin cardboard. Then hold the cardboard up so that sunlight shines through the holes and falls onto the white cardboard screen. Each little hole projects an image of the Sun, in just the same way that openings between the leaves on a tree do. An even simpler way is to crisscross the spaced fingers of one hand on top of the spaced fingers of your other hand and hold your hands over a screen. Sunlight shining between your fingers will also form the little crescents and other shapes of the Sun during the eclipse.

You also can use a pair of binoculars to project the Sun's image. Hold the binoculars' big end toward the Sun, about a foot away from the piece of white cardboard. Use the focusing knob to get a sharp image. Notice that the farther away from the cardboard screen you hold the binoculars, the bigger the Sun's image will be, but the dimmer it will be, too. You will see the image better if you shade it. Pasting your screen to the inside bottom of a cardboard box would provide good shade. You can, of course, use a telescope in the same way to project an image of the Sun onto a screen.

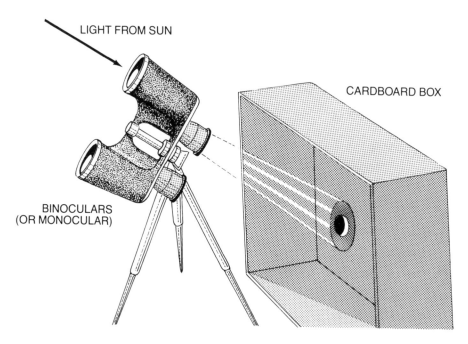

LIGHT FROM SUN

BINOCULARS
(OR MONOCULAR)

CARDBOARD BOX

A completely safe way to view an eclipse of the Sun is to project an image of the Sun onto a cardboard screen through binoculars. The diagram shows one way to mount binoculars to a tripod. The photograph shows the image the binoculars will project.

A word of warning when you use binoculars or a telescope for projection. The lenses usually are cemented into position, so if the instrument heats up too much you could seriously damage it. Let the Sun shine through the instrument for only brief periods of half a minute or so and then let it cool off.

You can keep a record of the eclipse by photographing the *projected image* at different stages. Any kind of camera will do. Make sure you photograph the image as head-on as you can. If you photograph it from off to one side, you will get an oval shape on the film. Since solar eclipses don't come around very often, it will be a good idea to get your equipment set up a couple of weeks ahead of time. That will give you a chance to shoot a trial roll of film and get it processed so that you can check your exposures. Film with an ASA speed of 100 or 200, and a camera with an automatic shutter-speed control, are fine for photographing projected images of the Sun.

Star Trails

Do the stars move? Does the Sun move? Of course they do, but not the way it seems to our eyes. We cannot see their real motions. Until around 1600, most people thought that our home planet was the center of the universe, and that Earth did not move. By day, they could see the Sun rise over the eastern horizon, climb across the sky, and set in the west. After an hour or so, the stars would twinkle into view. Like the Sun, they also appeared to parade across the sky from east to west. They were seen to move as a group, like soldiers on parade.

That motion of the Sun and stars across the sky is a trick motion and is not real. Astronomers call it apparent motion. As Earth turns on its axis, or rotates like a spinning top, we are carried around on its surface. And since Earth rotates clockwise, when we look up at the sky, everything there appears to be moving from east to west. But if Earth stopped rotating, the Sun and stars would no longer appear to move across the sky each day.

The stars actually do move in relation to each other, however. Then why don't we notice their motion? Because they are so very far away. Although they are traveling many miles a second, we cannot see their motion without special equipment. To someone on the ground, a high-flying aircraft will appear to move slowly, even though it may be going 500 miles an hour. Another aircraft that is moving along at the same speed but closer to us will appear to be going faster. The greater the distance of a moving object from our eyes, the slower it will appear to move. The stars are so distant that astronomers need very powerful telescopes and many years to observe a star change position.

Although you cannot photograph the actual motion of the stars, you can photograph their apparent motion and produce some lovely star trails. It is an easy thing to do and it is very satisfying.

TAKING STAR-TRAIL PHOTOGRAPHS

You will need a tripod, black-and-white or color film, and a camera that will let you make a time exposure. If you can see the North Star (Polaris) from where you live, you might start by photographing that part of the sky.

It's easy to find Polaris. First find the Big Dipper. Then use the two stars forming the Dipper's front edge as "pointer stars." Follow along the pointer stars and they will lead you straight to Polaris.

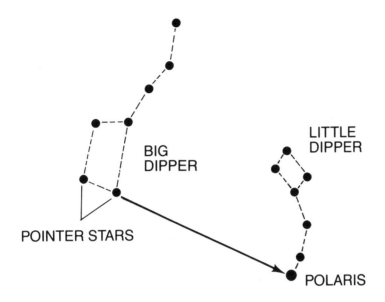

To find Polaris, the North Star, first find the Big Dipper. Then use the two stars forming the front edge of the dipper's bowl as "pointer stars" that point the way to Polaris.

Once you find Polaris, fix your camera to a tripod and aim the camera so that Polaris is in the middle of your viewfinder. Open the shutter and leave it open for at least 30 minutes. Try another exposure one hour long, and another 2 hours long. These photographs will show Polaris in a fixed position and all the other stars tracing arcs around it. If you have color film in your camera, you will even be able to see the different colors of the stars.

Over several nights of viewing, make exposures of different lengths and photograph different parts of the sky. Try exposures of 2, 5, 10, and 15 minutes. How do they differ from one another? Pick out a certain constellation and center it in your viewfinder. You might start a collection of star-trail constellations. The beauty of well-made star-trail photographs is very satisfying.

Star-trail photographs like this one are easy and fun to take. Set a camera on a tripod, aim it at a certain region of the sky, and make a long (1 to 2 hour) time exposure. (See text for exposure details.)

A bright Moon will light up the sky too much for taking good star-trail photographs. So will a horizon brightly lighted by city lights. The sky should be black and the air clear for best results. If you look through several back copies of the magazines *Sky and Telescope* and *Astronomy*, you will find many photographs taken by amateur astronomers. They usually tell what kind of film the photographer used and give the camera settings and exposure time.

9

VIEW FROM THE HIDDEN CITY

Suppose for a moment that you live in a city built in a huge hollow carved out of Earth's crustal rock and covered over by an enormous lid. Further suppose that the city rests on a huge elevator platform that can be raised to the surface and that the lid can slide back to expose the sky.

But the lid over the city is kept shut except for one night and one day every ten years. On that special night, the city is slowly raised to the surface and exposed to the natural sky. As it is raised, its lights are turned off. There is no work on this special day, no school. Not a single television set is left on, not a single restaurant, movie theater, or drive-in is open. Every office building is closed. Not so much as a candle flickers, for fear of spoiling the rare sight. When the city reaches the surface, every child and adult is entranced with the magnificence of the night. Many of the children have never experienced it before. For a long while no one speaks;

then the people begin excitedly to point out things they have observed—a meteor streak burning its way Earthward, the many colored stars twinkling brightly, the cloudy abundance of stars arching high across the sky as the Milky Way. Most of the people have binoculars, which reveal these splendors of the night in even more detail.

So grand and rare is their view that the people remain awake all night, except for some of the younger children who nod off to sleep now and then. Suddenly, a sliver of the Moon rises over the eastern horizon just before dawn. In only a few minutes, it is above the horizon as it glides westward. Those who have seen the real Moon before say that an even grander sight is to occur—the coming of day. Before long, the eastern sky gradually begins to grow light. In the process, the stars are snuffed out, the dimmer ones first, then the brighter ones. At first the eastern sky is pale gray, but as it brightens it glows yellow and then pink. By then, all but the brightest stars have been masked from view. But an especially bright one—someone says it is the planet Venus—is seen to rise over the eastern horizon. It announces the coming of the Sun, since that planet is known to move with the Sun. In the opposite direction, the sky is no longer black but has begun to fill with pale blue light. Then the top edge of the Sun pokes above the horizon and fills that part of the sky with red light. Some of the children are frightened and begin to cry. Within only a few minutes, the Sun has risen and continues its climb up the sky.

And still the people watch throughout the day. They watch clouds form and dissolve and see the sky change from a deep blue, to a pale blue, and then to blue-white as thin, high cirrus clouds move in. By late afternoon, the sky darkens as a storm builds. Dark clouds begin to rumble and crash and release rain. Once again the children are frightened, for it never rains when the city is safely below the ground. Just before sunset the rain stops, the sky clears, and a magnificent rainbow appears in the eastern sky. All but a few of the people have never seen a rainbow, and they cannot believe the wondrous thing they behold. Soon the rainbow fades as quickly as it came. As the Sun nears the horizon, the western sky and thin clouds there grow red, as does the Sun. For perhaps 20 minutes, the people are bathed in the orange-red light of the setting Sun. Then the sky once again grays and fades to dark. As it does, the brighter stars twinkle into view.

A great wailing siren now fills the city, the mournful sound filling every room and every heart, for the city has begun to lower back into its huge hollow within Earth's crust. As it does, the people return to their houses and apartments, and the artificial lights of the city—blue to imitate the natural sky—are turned on once again. Already the enormous lid has begun to close and eclipse the night sky. For another ten years, the lid will block the natural sky from view. No one understands why this must be so, but it has been for as long as the people can remember. To question why is forbidden.

The world around us indeed is "beautiful and mysterious," if only we can learn how to observe its many wonders. All of the things described in this book are ours—free for the looking and enjoying—not for only one day and one night every ten years but every night and every day. To let them slip by unnoticed is to miss part of life.

INDEX

ROY A. GALLANT, called "one of the deans of American science writers for children" by *School Library Journal*, is the author of more than sixty books on scientific subjects, including the best-selling National Geographic Society *Atlas of Our Universe*. Among his other books are *Private Lives of the Stars, 101 Questions and Answers about the Universe, The Macmillan Book of Astronomy*, and *The Constellations: How They Came to Be.*

Since 1979 Roy Gallant has been director of the Southworth Planetarium at the University of Southern Maine, where he holds an adjunct full professorship. He was previously a member of the faculty of the Hayden Planetarium in New York City and is a Fellow of the Royal Astronomical Society, London, and a member of the New York Academy of Sciences. He lives in Rangeley, Maine.